TUBTIME

by

ELVIRA WOODRUFF

illustrated by

SUÇIE STEVENSON

Holiday House / New York

Library of Congress Cataloging-in-Publication Data

Woodruff, Elvira.
    Tubtime / written by Elvira Woodruff : illustrated by Sucie
Stevenson.
        p.   cm.
    Summary: The O'Mally sisters' bubble bath has some scary moments
when they realize their bubbles contain chickens, frogs, and a mean,
hungry alligator.
    ISBN 0-8234-0777-2
    [1. Baths—Fiction.   2. Bubbles—Fiction.   3. Sisters—Fiction.]
I. Stevenson, Suçie, ill.   II. Title.
PZ7.W8606Tu   1990
[E]—dc20   89-36609   CIP   AC
ISBN 0-8234-0777-2

*For my sister, Shelly who's always muddy,
and my sister, Jen, who's always scrubbing.*
E.W.

For Claudia, Joe, and Ariel.
S.S.

The O'Mally sisters loved mud!

Marty liked to make mud cookies, mud pizzas, and all kinds of mud candy.

Maggie liked to build mud castles.

And Molly O'Mally loved to throw mud. She would throw it in the air and on the ground, and when no one was looking, at Murphy, her dog.

Unlike her children, Mrs. O'Mally had no love for mud at all. She hated it! When her girls came in from playing, she would take one look at them and say, "TUBTIME!"

So into the clean white bathroom the very muddy O'Mally sisters would march. They loved the tub almost as much as mud.

One day, when they came home muddier than ever, Mrs. O'Mally called to them from the kitchen, "Please start the tub while I answer the phone. I'll be right up." It was Aunt Minnie on the phone, and Aunt Minnie liked to talk!

"May we have bubbles?" Maggie called down the stairs.

"Be careful, not too many," Mrs. O'Mally answered.

"Minnie, I really must go now," Mrs. O'Mally said into the phone. But Aunt Minnie was describing her recipe for the "best tuna casserole you've ever tasted." She didn't want to hang up.

Marty poured the bubble bath into the water, and the three O'Mally sisters climbed in.

"Are you all in the tub? Is everything all right?" Mrs. O'Mally called up to them.

"Yes, we're all in the tub," Marty answered.

"And everything is fine and bubbly!" Maggie giggled.

"Hey, we forgot our new bubble pipes!" Marty
shouted. She climbed out of the tub and got them down
from the shelf.

The three sisters dipped their pipes into the bubbly water. Maggie threw a handful of suds at Molly, and it landed on her head.

"Hey, Molly looks like a chicken!" Maggie laughed. "Bauk, bauk, bauk!" Molly flapped her arms and pretended to be a chicken.

Then Molly blew into her bubble pipe. And she blew a bubble like no other bubble the O'Mally sisters had ever seen. It was a very big bubble, and it was full of chickens. Six squawking, wing-flapping chickens, to be exact!

The great chicken bubble wobbled this way and that.
It floated toward the sink. All the O'Mally sisters looked
at the giant bubble and then down at their pipes.

Suddenly they realized that these were no ordinary
bubble pipes. These were *extraordinary* bubble pipes!

"Frogs! How about some frogs! Little, leaping green frogs!" Marty grinned. She reached for her pipe and blew with all her might. Sure enough, the giant bubble coming out of Marty's pipe was full of frogs. Twelve high-jumping, long-leaping frogs!

"Oh, boy!" yelled Maggie. "How about an alligator? A big, fat, teeth-chomping alligator!"

She reached for her bubble pipe and blew the longest bubble yet. It was as long as the tub and was filled with the meanest, hungriest-looking alligator the O'Mally sisters had ever seen!

When the alligator saw the squawking chickens, he swished his powerful tail this way and that. Soon his great wobbling bubble was floating straight for the chickens.

Terrified, the chickens flapped their wings wildly. As their bubble wiggled and jiggled about the room, the alligator opened his giant mouth.

This set the chickens to pecking. They pecked and they pecked until finally they pecked their way right out of their bubble. Suddenly there were chickens everywhere, and the O'Mally bathroom was a sea of fluttering feathers.

It didn't take the chickens long to peck a hole in the frogs' bubble. Frogs began leaping over feathers, and feathers began flying over frogs. And everyone was trying to stay away from the alligator!

Downstairs, Mrs. O'Mally was still on the phone with Aunt Minnie.

"Yes, Minnie, I do want to hear about your vacation, but I must check on my girls." She held out the phone as she called up the stairs.

"Are you all in the tub? Is everything all right up there?"

"Yes, we're all in the tub," Maggie called down.
"But everything is not really all right!" Marty whispered as she peeked over the edge.

The alligator was now the only one left in a bubble, and he was not very happy. As he floated past the tub, the three little O'Mallys sank down into the suds. The alligator grinned as he headed for the hook next to the shower.

"Oh, no!" cried Marty.

"He's going to break his bubble!" cried Maggie.

"Quick, the window!" called Marty. "Open the window!" In a flash the three O'Mallys were out of the tub, slipping and sliding their way across the floor.

They opened the window and the frogs, feeling a cool breeze, leapt up and out. In a great flurry of feathers, the chickens followed the frogs.

But the alligator was still in his bubble, quietly circling the room. He looked down at the little O'Mallys and then over to the large hook on the wall. He had a hopeful look in his eye. Actually it was a very hopeful and hungry look. For it was well past his dinner time.

Suddenly, there were footsteps on the stairs. It was
Mr. O'Malley, who had come home from work.
"Bathtime's over!" he called
"No!" cried Molly.

"Quick! The window!" cried Marty.
The three little O'Malleys leapt out of the tub.
They pushed the alligator right out the window
just as their father came in.

"Are they all in the tub? Is everything all right?" Mrs. O'Mally called up to her husband.

"Yes, they're all in the tub," Mr. O'Mally called down. "But it looks like a herd of elephants has been through this bathroom!" He sighed.

When Marty, Maggie, and Molly heard this, they looked at each other and grinned!

"Will you blow us a bubble, Dad?" Maggie asked.

"Well, all right, but just one," Mr. O'Mally said as he picked up a bubble pipe from the floor.

"Should I make it a big one?" he asked, as he put the pipe to his mouth.

"Oh, yes!" squealed the three little O'Mallys. "It will have to be a very big bubble!" they giggled, as they dove under the suds to hide.

Meanwhile, downstairs, Mrs. O'Mally was still on the phone with Aunt Minnie. As the ceiling shook like thunder overhead, Mrs. O'Mally just closed her eyes and smiled.

"Yes Minnie, it's all right. You can go ahead and tell me all about it. That noise? Oh, that's probably just my girls. They must all be out of the tub." She smiled.